W9-DEL-105

ANIMAL ANTICS A TO Z®

Oliver Otter's Own Office

by Barbara deRubertis • illustrated by R.W. Alley

THE KANE PRESS / NEW YORK

Alpha Betty's Class

Alexander Anteater

Bobby Baboon

Corky Cub

Dilly Dog

Eddie Elephant

Frances Frog

Gertie Gorilla

Hanna Hippo

Izzy Impala

Jeremy Jackrabbit

Kylie Kangaroo

Lana Llama

Maxwell Moose

Nina Nandu
STAR of the BOOK
Oliver Otter
Polly Porcupine
Quentin Quokka
Rosie Raccoon
Sammy Skunk
Tessa Tiger
Umma Ungka
Victor Vicuna
Walter Warthog
Xavier Ox
Yoko Yak
Zachary Zebra
Alpha Betty

Library of Congress Cataloging-in-Publication Data

deRubertis, Barbara.
Oliver Otter's own office / by Barbara deRubertis ; illustrated by R.W. Alley.
p. cm. — (Animal antics A to Z)
Summary: Oliver Otter's little sister and brother are always ruining his homework until their parents make Oliver his very own office.
ISBN 978-1-57565-336-5 (library binding : alk. paper) — ISBN 978-1-57565-327-3 (pbk. : alk. paper)
[1. Brothers and sisters—Fiction. 2. Homework—Fiction. 3. Otters—Fiction. 4. Alphabet.]
I. Alley, R. W. (Robert W.), ill. II. Title.
PZ7.D4475Ol 2011
[E]—dc22 2010025288

1 3 5 7 9 10 8 6 4 2

First published in the United States of America in 2011 by Kane Press, Inc.
Printed in the United States of America
WOZ0111

Series Editor: Juliana Hanford
Book Design: Edward Miller

www.kanepress.com

Oliver Otter was having homework problems at Alpha Betty's school.

Sometimes he turned in homework that had holes poked in it.

Sometimes his homework
was soaking wet.

Sometimes his homework
was torn.

And sometimes his
homework got lost.

"Oh, dear!" said Alpha Betty when Oliver gave her MORE torn homework.

Oliver looked down at his toes.
"I'm sorry," he told Alpha Betty.

When Oliver arrived home that afternoon, his room was a mess.

His whole cottage was a mess!

And Oliver knew why.

Opal and Otto, the twins, were toddlers.

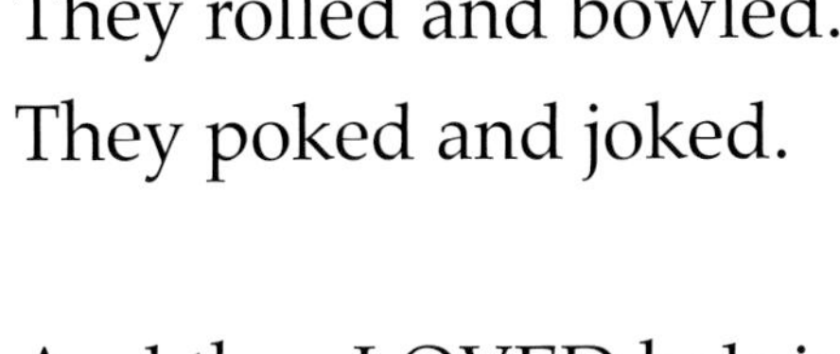

They hopped and bopped.
They rolled and bowled.
They poked and joked.

And they LOVED helping Oliver with his homework!

Oliver spoke slowly to the twins.

“Look. I have FOUR pages of homework.
I do not want them to get poked.
Or soaked. Or torn. Or lost!”

Opal and Otto nodded.

Oliver tried to do homework on the sofa.

But it got poked.

"So sowwy!" said Opal.

He tried to do homework on the floor.

But it got soaked.

"So sowwy!" said Otto.

He tried to do homework on his cot.

But it got torn.

"So sowwy!" said Opal and Otto as they ran off in opposite directions.

And Oliver could not even FIND his last page of homework!

The next day, Oliver gave his homework to Alpha Betty.

One page was poked. One page was soaked. One page was torn. And one page was lost.

So Alpha Betty gave Oliver a note to take home.

Mom and Pop read the note.
"Oh, Oliver!" they said. "What shall we do?"

Oliver had been thinking it over.
And he had an idea. He was hoping
he could have his own office.

Both Mom and Pop did.

Mom had her office on the boat dock by the pond.

She sold boats and oars she made of oak.

Pop had his office near his big outdoor stove.

He sold hot rolls fresh from the oven.

But Oliver had no office.
He could not even close the door to his room.

There was no door!

Tears plopped onto Oliver's overalls.

"I need my own office," he sobbed.
"You both have offices for your jobs.

My job is school. I need an office where
I can do my homework."

Mom and Pop looked at each other.

Then Mom said, "Jolly good idea!"
And Pop said, "Let's go to work!"

Oliver hopped up and down.
"O–KAY!" he shouted.

Pop bought a door for Oliver's room.

Mom made him a desk of solid oak.

And Oliver set up everything just the way he wanted it.

On Monday, Oliver brought home four more pages of homework.
He closed his office door.

And for the first time, he did four pages of NEAT homework.

Opal and Otto could not poke it.
Or soak it. Or tear it. Or lose it!

They sat on the floor by Oliver's door.
They were oddly quiet.
And they looked a little sad.

The following morning, Oliver proudly gave his homework to Alpha Betty.

"Bravo!" she shouted. "You have solved your homework problem!"

"YES!" Oliver smiled. "I have my own office now!"

But something was bothering Oliver.
He thought about it all afternoon.

Oliver jogged home after school.
And he went straight to his office to do his homework.

Opal and Otto sat on the floor by his door.
They spoke ever so softly. "Ow-wiv-errr!
We have nothing to doooo!"

Oliver frowned.
He had solved his homework problem.
But now he had a toddler problem!

Then an idea popped into his head. . . .

Oliver was excited as he set to work on his plan.
He cut holes in boxes to make desks.
He found lots of crayons and paper.
Then he put a toy phone on top of each desk.

"Now you have offices, too!" he told the twins.

The happy twins phoned Oliver right away. “Tanks, Owwiver!” they said.

Opal, Otto, and Oliver LOVED their new offices. And Oliver Otter’s homework was never poked, or soaked, or torn, or lost again!

STAR OF THE BOOK: THE OTTER

FUN FACTS

- Home: Otters are found everywhere in the world—except Australia. They like to spend most of their time in the water.
- Appearance: Otters are built for swimming! They have slender bodies, tapered tails, short legs, and webbed feet.
- Size: River otters are about 3 to 4 feet long, from nose to tail tip, and can weigh up to 30 pounds. Sea otters can be 5 feet long and weigh 100 pounds!
- **Did You Know?** Otters love to play! They enjoy sliding down mud or snow banks, playing "follow the leader," and chasing their friends!

LOOK BACK

Learning to identify letter sounds (phonemes) at the beginning, middle, and end of words is called "phonemic awareness."

- The word *top* has a *short o* sound. Listen to the words on page 8 being read again. When you hear a word that has the *short o* sound, put your hands on top of your head and say the word!
- The word *toes* has a *long o* sound. Listen to page 9 being read again. When you hear a word that has the *long o* sound, touch your toes and say the word!
- **BONUS!** Now it's time for double trouble! Listen to page 17 being read again. Put your hands on top of your head when you hear a *short o* sound and touch your toes when you hear a *long o* sound!

TRY THIS!

Make Words with Oliver's Oranges

- Draw nine oranges on a sheet of paper.* Lightly color the oranges. Then cut them out.
- Write a **red *o*** on one orange. Write a **green consonant** (*c, d, g, h, l, n, p*) on each of seven oranges. Write a **black *t*** on one orange.
- Make three-letter words with a **green consonant** at the beginning, the **red *o*** in the middle, and the **black *t*** at the end. Sound out each word!
- **JUST FOR FUN:** Deal out the oranges into three piles for Opal, Otto, and Oliver. How many oranges does each one get?

*A printable, ready-to-use activity page with nine oranges is available at: www.kanepress.com/AnimalAntics/OliverOtter.html

(The words you can make: cot, dot, got, hot, lot, not, pot)

FOR MORE ACTIVITIES, go to Oliver Otter's website: www.kanepress.com/AnimalAntics/OliverOtter.html
You'll also find a recipe for Oliver Otter's Orange-Cranberry Oatmeal Scones!